Legs

A Who's-
Under-the-
Flap Book

Little Simon

"My big long legs
will make you laugh."
These are the legs
of a spotted . . .

"I sing songs
that I'm sure
you've heard."
These skinny legs
are the legs of a . . .

"My legs look skinny
because my body's so big."
These legs belong
to a curly-tailed . . .

"My legs run very fast,
of course."
These speedy legs
are the legs of a . . .

"I have lots of legs
and they're just what I need."
Who has all these legs?
It's a long . . .

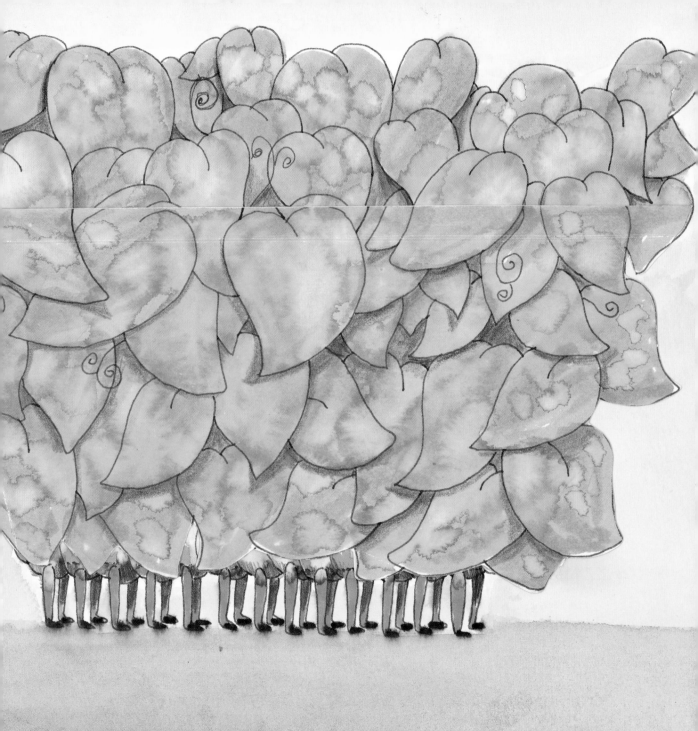

"I walk on my legs
but my claws like to grab."
These bumpy legs
are the legs of a . . .

"A girl ran away
when I sat down beside her."
These eight legs
are the legs of a . . .

"My legs are covered
with long white hair."
These legs belong to a big . . .

"Jump, jump, jump!
That's what my legs do."
These are the legs of a bouncy . . .

Hey, look! Some more legs—
Lined up two-by-two.
Whose legs are these?
That's easy, it's . . .

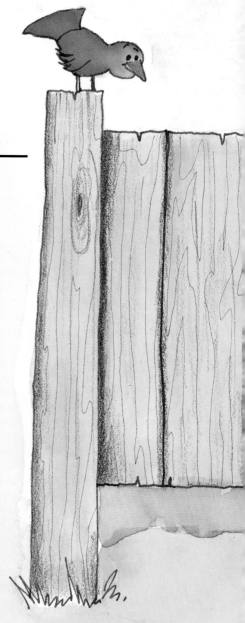